LITTLE KOALA

by Margaret Roc
illustrated by Deborah Brown

Angus&Robertson
An imprint of HarperCollins*Publishers*

Little Koala wanted to draw a picture.
'What will I draw?' she wondered.

'Draw the most beautiful animal in the bush,'
said her friend. 'Draw me.'

So Little Koala did.

4

'What are you doing?' asked the frill-necked lizard.

'I'm drawing the most beautiful animal in the bush,'
said Little Koala.

'But where is his frill-neck?' asked the frill-necked lizard.
'You will have to draw his frill-neck.'

So Little Koala did.

'What are you doing?' asked the emu.

'I'm drawing the most beautiful animal in the bush,' said Little Koala.

'But where are her long legs?' asked the emu.
'You will have to draw her long legs.'

11

So Little Koala did.

'What are you doing?' asked the cockatoo.

'I'm drawing the most beautiful animal in the bush,' said Little Koala.

'But where is his yellow crest?' asked the cockatoo.
'You will have to draw his yellow crest.'

So Little Koala did.

'What are you doing?' asked the wallaby.

'I'm drawing the most beautiful animal in the bush,'
said Little Koala.

'But where is her big tail?' asked the wallaby.
'You will have to draw her big tail.'

So Little Koala did.

'What are you doing?' asked the kookaburra.

'I'm drawing the most beautiful animal in the bush,' said Little Koala.

22

'But where are her wings?' asked the kookaburra.
'You will have to draw her wings.'

So Little Koala did.

'What are you doing?' asked the echidna.

'I'm drawing the most beautiful animal in the bush,' said Little Koala.

'But where are his spines?' asked the echidna.
'You will have to draw his spines.'

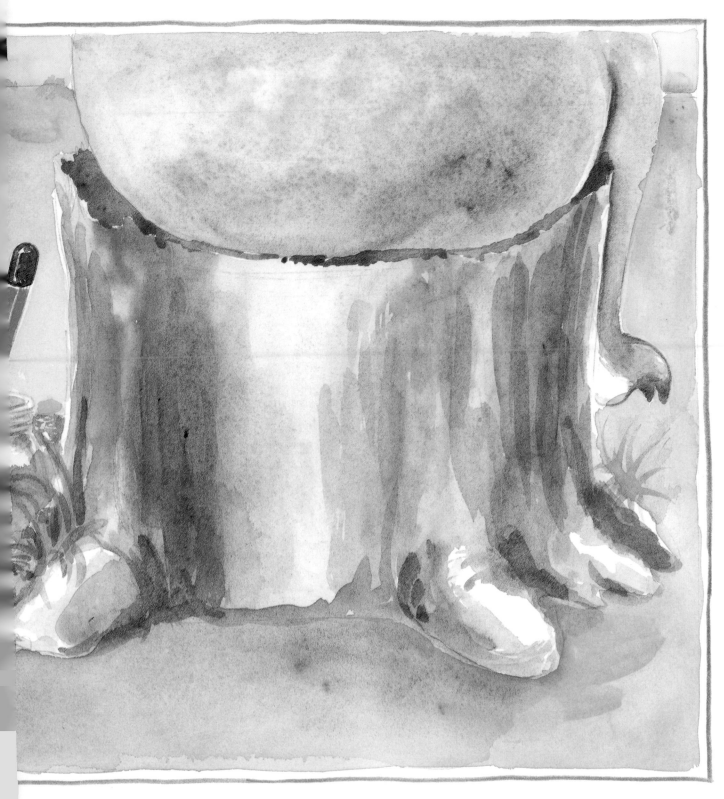

So Little Koala did.

'There you are,' said Little Koala to her friend.
'The most beautiful animal in the bush,'

'Oh! That's not me,' said her friend.
'That must be a bunyip.'

And all the animals
laughed and laughed.

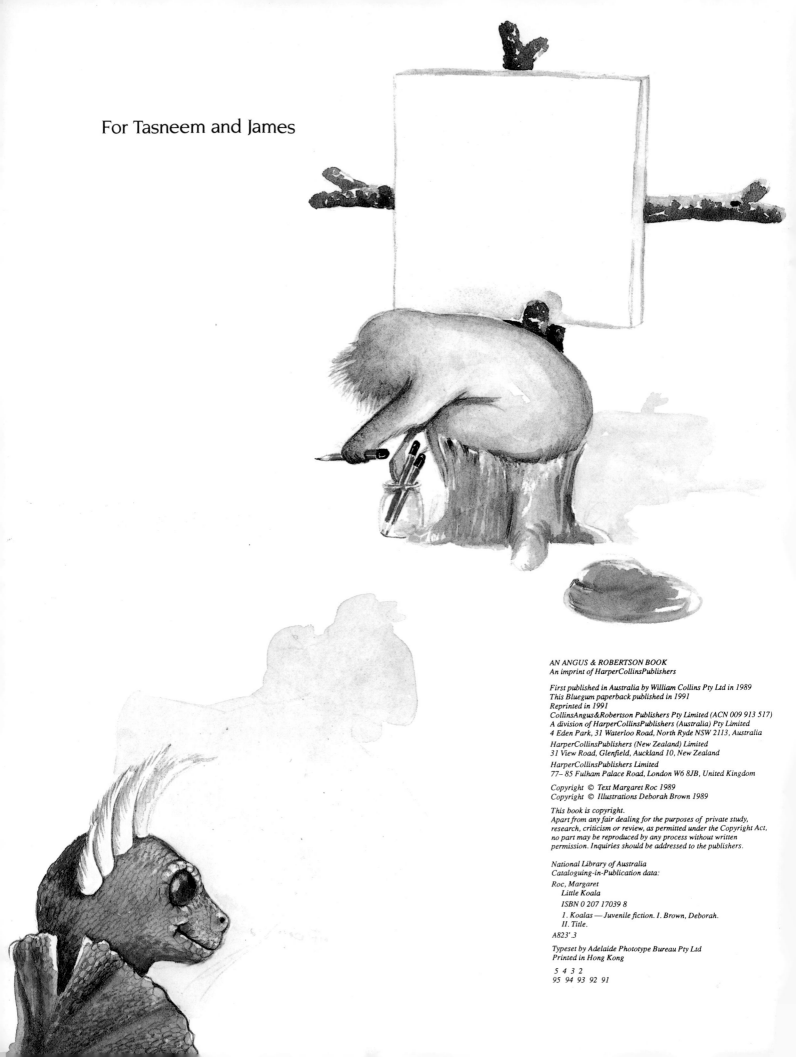

For Tasneem and James

AN ANGUS & ROBERTSON BOOK
An imprint of HarperCollinsPublishers

First published in Australia by William Collins Pty Ltd in 1989
This Bluegum paperback published in 1991
Reprinted in 1991
CollinsAngus&Robertson Publishers Pty Limited (ACN 009 913 517)
A division of HarperCollinsPublishers (Australia) Pty Limited
4 Eden Park, 31 Waterloo Road, North Ryde NSW 2113, Australia
HarperCollinsPublishers (New Zealand) Limited
31 View Road, Glenfield, Auckland 10, New Zealand
HarperCollinsPublishers Limited
77– 85 Fulham Palace Road, London W6 8JB, United Kingdom

Copyright © Text Margaret Roc 1989
Copyright © Illustrations Deborah Brown 1989

National Library of Australia
Cataloguing-in-Publication data:
Roc, Margaret
  Little Koala
  ISBN 0 207 17039 8
    1. Koalas — Juvenile fiction. I. Brown, Deborah.
    II. Title.
A823'.3

Typeset by Adelaide Phototype Bureau Pty Ltd
Printed in Hong Kong

 5 4 3 2
95 94 93 92 91